THE MANY SELVES OF ANN-ELIZABETH

For Charisa.

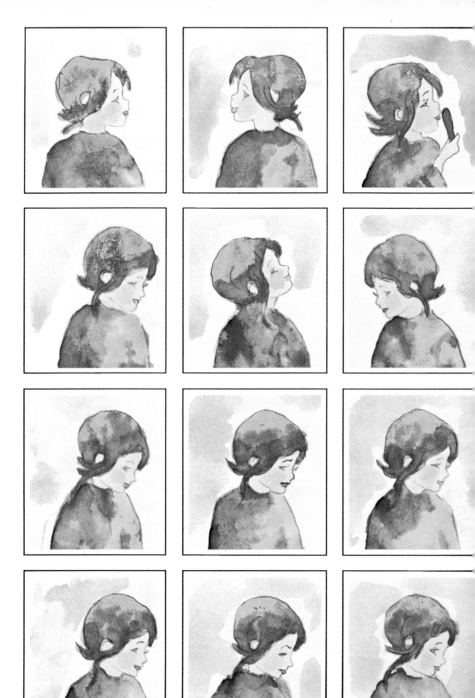

THE MANY SELVES OF ANN-ELIZABETH

By Evelyn Maples

Illustrations by Charlene Loeding

6- 11 - 75

Copyright © 1973

Independence Press
Box 1019
Independence, Missour

Library of Congress Catalog Card No. 72-95452

ISBN-0-8309-0093-4

Printed in the United States of America

A Note from the Author

This book began not with the author but with the artist. One beautiful spring day an editor plopped a packet on my desk and said, "Here are some illustrations I know you'll just love! How about writing a story to go along with them?"

The editor was right. I did love the illustrations. They had a delicate, old-English look, and the deft blending of watercolors indicated an artist of no small talent. And then I heard her story.

Charlene Loeding was born October 4, 1945, in Port Huron, Michigan, and reared in a warm, loving family who nourished her interest in art, books, and people. In college she chose to combine these interests in the field of library science. She had worked for seven months as a school librarian when she was killed in an automobile accident in the spring of 1970.

It was Charlene's mother, Mrs. Russell Loeding, who brought the illustrations to my friend the editor. It was her wish that they be used in some way to enhance the lives of children, a fitting memorial to her beautiful, gentle daughter.

For three months I daily shuffled the illustrations and searched for a story line. The theme of self-acceptance which evolved was suggested, of course, by the illustrations themselves and is psychologically sound according to modern behavioral scientists. Maurice Nicoll, in **Psychological Commentaries**, has said: "When a man begins to observe himself from the angle that he is not one but many, he begins to work on his being."

It was my pleasure to put the words to the "music."

Evelyn Maples

Ann-Elizabeth sat at the table and pouted. She did not like her red hair. She did not like her big house. She did not like being Ann-Elizabeth. She had quarreled with her friend Judy and had told her to go home. ("You have ugly red hair and I don't like you," Judy had said as she ran out the door.) Unhappy Ann-Elizabeth had kicked Kitty Blue when Kitty tried to make her feel better. (Kitty Blue had voiced one sharp "Meow" and limped to her basket.) Naughty Ann-Elizabeth made a face at her mother when her mother asked her to clean her room. ("Very well," Mother had said. "I don't mind your room being dirty. I like mine clean!") Ann-Elizabeth felt like a cross, ugly monster.

Ann-Elizabeth climbed the stairs and looked out
her bedroom window. The sky was gloomy. The garden was gloomy.
Ann-Elizabeth was gloomy too. Suddenly Ann-Elizabeth made up her mind.
She would be someone else!

She ran down the stairs and out onto the road.
There she met a washerwoman. "Please, Mrs. Washerwoman, may I be your
little girl?" she asked. "I don't like being Ann-Elizabeth."

Two heads popped up in the wheelbarrow the washerwoman was pushing.
"I'm sorry, Ann-Elizabeth," the woman said. "You cannot
be my little girl. Two children are quite enough for a poor washerwoman."

Ann-Elizabeth wandered into the woods.
There she saw a beautiful partridge. "Please, Mrs. Partridge, may I be your
little partridge? I don't like being Ann-Elizabeth."

"I'm sorry, Ann-Elizabeth," said Mrs. Partridge.
"You cannot be my little partridge. Seven young ones are quite enough to
care for in these woods." And Mrs. Partridge
and her seven little partridges strolled off in single file.

Ann-Elizabeth sat down on a stump and thought and thought. As she
thought she realized that she was many Ann-Elizabeths.
There was the dancing Ann-Elizabeth, the thoughtful Ann-Elizabeth, the helpful
Ann-Elizabeth, the pouting Ann-Elizabeth, the friendly
Ann-Elizabeth—and several more.

And she must not forget the monster Ann-Elizabeth.
That cross, ugly Ann-Elizabeth had come into the woods with her too.
Perhaps being red-haired-Ann-Elizabeth-of-many-selves
was really not too bad.
Perhaps—just perhaps—she should go back home and try again.

As Ann-Elizabeth came near her home everything looked different somehow—sunshiny and clean and new.

She hurried to the door

and into the dining room.
There all the Ann-Elizabeths played until they were tired.

Then they went into the library for tea and talk.
Quiet Ann-Elizabeth explained to shy Ann-Elizabeth that sometimes
she liked being alone. Dancing Ann-Elizabeth and
happy Ann-Elizabeth did a waltz around the room just for fun.
Tired Ann-Elizabeth sat on a stool and
watched—that is, until dancing Ann-Elizabeth stepped on her toe.

Then a peculiar thing happened.
The monster Ann-Elizabeth came stomping up the hall—but she was smiling
in a halfhearted way. Ann-Elizabeth decided she could love
and accept the monster too.

Helpful Ann-Elizabeth put on her mother's apron and dust cap
and swept and dusted until everything
looked just right.   She thought the house should be tidy at bedtime.
Mother would be glad too.

Ann-Elizabeth laughed out loud when she opened the door to her room. There on the bed lay monster Ann-Elizabeth's pajamas. She wouldn't need those tonight. She was content to be just Ann-Elizabeth. Ann-Elizabeth, who was many Ann-Elizabeths at the same time she was red-haired-Ann-Elizabeth-who-lived-in-the-big-house, pulled the covers up around her. "I <u>like</u> being Ann-Elizabeth," she said. And soon she was fast asleep.

SOMETIMES PEOPLE ARE GOOD

1. Some - times peo - ple are good, And they do just what they should,
   But the ver - y same peo - ple who are good some - times Are the ver - y same peo - ple who are bad some - times. It's fun - ny but it's

2. Some - times peo - ple get wet, And their par - ents get up - set.
   But the ver - y same peo - ple who get wet some - times Are the ver - y same peo - ple who are dry some - times. It's fun - ny but it's